Praise for S.D. Hint

"Vivid, kick-ass horror--just plain recommended."

-- John Shirley, author of *Bleak House*

"S.D. Hintz…does not disappoint, seamlessly weaving people and place into a tapestry that intrigues almost as much as it chills."

-- *Horror Bound Magazine*

"Hintz's novelette is a fun mix of Stephen King's NEEDFUL THINGS and Tim Lebbon's ASSASSIN series."

-- *The Horror Fiction Review*

"Hintz…made me shudder and laugh simultaneously."

-- *Horror World*

"A perfect tale to tell during a campfire."

-- *You Gotta Read Reviews*

S.D. Hintz

STARVELINGS

S.D. Hintz

S.D. Hintz

FIRST EDITION

Starvelings

Published by Aristotle Books

This book is a work of fiction.
Names, characters, places, and incidents either are the product of the author's imagination or are used fictitiously. Any resemblance to actual persons, living or dead, events, or locales is entirely coincidental.

To Ashanti and my circle of friends,

who have always believed in this wicked tale

S.D. Hintz

CHAPTER ONE

"Mom? Can I go now?"

"Where's the big, white one I asked you to get? C'mon! Hop to it!"

"Aw!"

Parker Paget whirled on the living room, oblivious to his mom drowning in a sea of cardboard boxes. He then dashed out the front door like his Nikes were on fire. He knew his mom had the unpacking under control, so he wasn't about to suggest a helping hand. Besides, she would just end up yelling at him for getting in the way or disorganizing the various housewares. He figured she would rather he stayed out of her hair.

"Parker! Bring Maggie with you!"

He stopped in his tracks at the doorstep. "Here, girl!"

Maggie, their Golden Labrador Retriever, leapt out of the shadows from behind the couch. She spotted her best friend at the other side of the living room, and wondered how she would reach him through the clutter. She whined longingly.

Parker slapped his hands twice on his thighs. "C'mon!"

S.D. Hintz

Maggie barked and lost all sensibility. She was like a cruise missile, locking her sights and launching at her target. She cleared the couch in two jumps and the boxes in one, landing gracefully in the foyer at Parker's feet. He smiled while his mom rolled her eyes and shook her head. He patted Maggie's side and they headed out the door.

The crisp, fragrant breeze tickled Parker's nose; it was an odd potpourri of his surroundings - eucalyptus, pine needles, and chokeberry – reminiscent of baby powder and cough drops. It also triggered instant flashbacks of camping in the Boundary Waters with his dad. Fishing for bass and catching basswood. Pitching a tent too close to the campfire. Hiking off-trail and getting lost. Parker's dad was far from a man's man; he was a bestselling horror author, a bit of a patsy when it came to wilderness excursions and home repairs. He was great at writing a plan and putting it into inaction, chocking up number twenty on the proverbial honey do list. But what else would you expect from a guy glued to his laptop twelve hours a day?

A dust cloud trailed Parker across the gravel drive as he rounded the silver Lexus CT. The hatchback was still open, and Maggie leapt up with her front paws on the bumper, sniffing the

8

car's interior curiously. Parker joined her side and grabbed the last remaining box. It was the heaviest one yet, filling his arms to his chin. It was probably jam-packed with his dad's precious *Encyclopedia Britannica* library. He grunted and headed back up the drive, with Maggie one step ahead, doing his best to ignore the dull ache that slowly coursed from his shoulders on down.

His gaze wandered over their new house. He had never seen one like it before. Its saltbox frame and red cedar siding gave it the facade of a bloody skull. The cobwebbed eaves were concave with rusted gutters that looked like bloodstained machetes. Twisted black walnuts crowded the drive, casting the front lawn in spidery shadows. Without a doubt, it was a homestead made for a horror author.

Parker bounded the doorstep and dropped the box into the foyer. It landed hard, sounding like a gunshot.

Muriel jumped, and then sighed upon glimpsing her eager son. "Be back by six for supper!"

"I will!"

Parker ran out of the house before his mom could bark another order. There was only so much sunlight in a day. They had spent the morning cleaning out their condo and packing up the car. Most of the afternoon they road-tripped, burning the tar a good three and a half hours to their new house. Before long, nightfall would be creeping towards the horizon.

As exciting as the thought of exploring a different world was, the anxiety of attending a new school swirled in Parker's subconscious. He had been in the seventh grade two months, in the same district his entire life, and even though it had been a few days since he had said his goodbyes, his heart ached at having to leave his friends behind. Rory, Jersey, Nash, all those guys. No more playing Army in the backwoods, touch football in the vacant lot, or clowning around in Sunset Park. That life was gone, dead. Now he had to start over, make new friends, and be the odd man out. It sucked. More so, it was troubling how one person's impulsive decision could destroy another's happiness.

Parker had been struggling the past couple nights in bed to find an iota of forgiveness in his heart. Was it his dad's fault that one of his novels topped the *New York Times Bestseller List*? No, yet it failed to support a valid reason to relocate the family to the other side of the state. His dad had said that an isolated residence would enable him to write horror more effectively, something about nature's ambiance. He understood that his dad was the provider, seeing how his mom had become a housewife after ten high-stress years as a nurse, but why was it all about him? Parker knew he could spend hours on end searching for an answer and would only conjure more questions. So, he continued to tell himself that his dad had a logical rationale.

"C'mon, Maggie!"

Maggie lingered on the doorstep, as if uncertain she had permission to play with her friend. She bolted at the sound of her name and kept pace with Parker. He ducked beneath the black walnuts, headed alongside the house, and then stumbled over a stump into the backyard.

He caught his breath as he soaked in his unfamiliar surroundings. It was obvious the groundskeeper had taken the year off. The lawn was green with crabgrass and sandbur. A single, gnarled oak swayed subtly like a skyscraper, struggling to shade the entire yard. To Parker's left was a withered vegetable garden, choked with weeds and entangled in brown netting. In the distance, twenty meters or so ahead, a red footbridge spanned a brook that meandered into a dense grove.

Maggie paused briefly beside Parker, until her nose got the best of her. She trotted across the yard, sniffing everything at her front paws. Parker picked up a stick and followed close behind, dueling an imaginary pirate. Lately, he had abandoned *Star Wars* for *Raiders of the Seven Seas*, transforming his lightsaber into a cutlass.

"Yah, matey! Avast ye!"

Parker lunged and spun across the lawn, slicing his stick through the air. Maggie found her own war to wage and paused to urinate on a fallen bird's nest. Parker took the lead as the breeze enlivened dead leaves, rolling them like a wave across his shoes. He swiped at them, pretending they were octopus tentacles. He glanced over his shoulder. Maggie sprinted past him, paranoid of being left behind.

Both friends stopped at the small bridge. It was a wreck of a structure. The wood floorboards were splintered and the red paint had flaked in splotches. The railing wobbled and creaked in the wind. If the bridge had been any larger, Parker would have passed and found a way around it. But, seeing how he could span it in a mere five steps, he figured he would give it a shot.

He stepped onto the planks and they moaned beneath his weight. Maggie stood on solid ground and looked up at him, reluctant to follow. He leaned slightly over the railing, careful not to touch it in fear it would collapse, and gazed at the brook below. It bubbled over smooth, peach-sized stones, twigs and fallen leaves. The water looked cold and the breeze sent a shiver through Parker's sweatshirt. He regarded Maggie, wondering if she felt the same; she was more than acclimated, using the brook as her own personal fountain. He figured he would venture beyond the bridge a bit, see if there was anything of interest, and then turn back before he caught the sniffles.

The planks sighed as he stepped onto solid ground. Maggie leapt over the bridge, refusing to chance it, and joined his side. Before him, within the grove, elms and ashes swayed, scraping branches, sounding like razors on strops. The dead grass was buried ankle-deep with piles of leaves; it reminded Parker of winter and the snow banks formed by the plows. Grinning, he charged forward, kicking and crunching through nature's blanket. Maggie hopped around behind him, attempting to snatch the floating leaves in her jaws.

Parker paused to catch his breath as a gust scattered the piles more so. Maggie zigzagged back and forth, panting and pawing, refusing to forfeit the game. Parker scanned the grove. Where they stood now, heavy shadows encompassed them, wavering as if alive. Except for the wind, which had picked up to a howl, their surroundings were silent. He ventured forth, wide-eyed and watchful, hoping to God he was not in bear country.

"Maggie!"

His protector matched his pace and his fear subsided slightly. He was glad his mom told him to bring the dog. Otherwise, by this time, he would have run for the hills. But with Maggie by his side, he was more apt to extend his exploration.

Parker recalled asking his dad during the road trip about the lot. His response encouraged him: *There's some woods out back, and an old farm somewhere beyond that. At least that's what our agent said.*

A twig snapped.

Parker dropped his stick and bolted like a track athlete at the sound of a starting gun. In his mind's eye, a black bear nipped at his heels. Maggie dashed ahead, determined to win the race, just as she had the other day at the park.

The setting sun blinded Parker as he emerged from the grove. He used his right palm as a visor and looked over his shoulder. As far as he could see into the grove, nothing pursued them. No bears, no squirrels, nothing.

Maggie plopped down on the ground for a breather, tongue lolling and tail wagging. Parker was out of breath and his side ached. He followed Maggie's suggestion and sat beside her. He squinted beneath his palm. A three-foot high wood utility fence defined the property line. On the other side was an acre-expanse of dirt, mole hills and crabgrass. The magenta horizon silhouetted a dilapidated, crimson barn with a green gambrel roof.

That must be the old farm Dad mentioned, Parker thought, lowering his hand.

His curiosity peaked. He had never set foot on a farm before, let alone entered a barn. And as far as he could tell, from his vantage point, the structure was abandoned. There was not a house or silo in accompaniment. It was possible the farm was so old that the other buildings had long since collapsed. But if that was true, there would be piles of wreckage. All Parker saw was the barn. He needed a closer look.

He checked his tennis shoes. Just as he had expected. The laces were covered in burs. Wincing, he picked each one off and flicked it aside. He then stood and brushed off his jeans. He approached the utility fence and climbed over it in two steps and a straddle.

"C'mon, girl!"

Maggie hopped up and ducked beneath the lowest crossbeam. Once across the property line, she shook her body as if soaked to the bone, convinced the fence had dirtied her fur. Moments later, she realized she was trailing and bolted like a cheetah after a gazelle. She flew past Parker with her sights set on the barn. He watched her kick up dust, his heart drumming with a snare's tempo, begging him to slow his pace.

A gust tousled his hair and knocked him back a step. He raised his arm, squinting beneath his makeshift visor. Maggie had stopped a safe distance from the barn, stretching forward and sniffing. Still curious, she crept up to the double doors.

I wonder what she smells, Parker thought. *Can't be anything in there but dust and hay.*

With his heartbeat regulated, he resorted to squinting and trotted the remaining length of the field. He eyed the barn, as its striking details became apparent. The roof looked leprous; the asphalt shingles were either missing or peeling near the eaves. The three visible, narrow windows were cracked and cloudy as swamp water. The hayloft was a pitch-black cavern, protected with a barbed wire mesh. Below, the double doors were ajar and banged in the wind, held fast by a rusted chain on the handles.

Parker looked to Maggie, who was now within earshot. Her tailed wagged as she poked her nose between the doors.

That was when Parker heard her growl.

"Maggie! Out! Over here!"

He was maybe five yards from the doors when the stench hit him. It smelled like spoiled hamburger, as if a cow or horse had died within. Maggie retracted her nose and turned toward Parker. She took a step forward.

The double doors banged, and jutted out, clanking the chain. An emaciated, chalk-white arm shot out of the darkness. Maggie jumped and barked in surprise, yet never saw it coming. A skeletal hand with long bloodstained fingers clutched her right hock and yanked her back. She yelped and thrashed about.

"Maggie!"

Parker lunged for her front paws. Landing on his stomach, he grabbed them, and found himself in a tug-of-war over his best friend. He held her tight and planted his feet, but soon realized that the sickly *thing* within the barn was ten times stronger. A *thing* or a *man*? The size of the hands seemed masculine. Still, the rest of its body remained cloaked in darkness.

Can't...hold on...much longer, Parker thought.

Maggie whined as her paws slipped through his grip. Her puppy-dog eyes pleaded for his comfort, and apologized for her curiosity. Parker gritted his teeth and shook his head.

The thing behind the doors hissed.

Maggie yelped as her left foreleg dislocated.

Parker's face twisted in horror. "No!"

The canine rope suddenly cut some slack, as if the thing in the barn tired of the struggle. Parker, careful not to hurt Maggie further, tried to slide his hands up to her collar, hoping to grab it for more leverage. The moment he let go of her limbs, she was jerked out of his grasp. Her body slammed into the double doors, booming like a battering ram.

Parker shrieked, scrambling to his feet. "Maggie! Let her go! You let her go!"

Maggie crashed into the doors again, horizontally, like a *Tetris* piece forced to block a vertical space.

She was sprawled on the ground, corpse-still, blood cascading down her face. She whimpered and locked gazes with Parker, glassy-eyed. He stood, frozen in disbelief, knowing he had to help her, but uncertain how to proceed. His only thought was to grab her and drag her as far away as possible, across the field and back home. He hesitated, though, not wanting to subject her to another violent tug-of-war.

He eyed the splintered doors. In the six-inch gap, dark as a crevasse, nothing moved, or hissed. And as pale as the skin was on the thing inside, Parker failed to spot a speck of white. He looked at the chain; it dangled and shifted slightly, tickled by the wind.

Just grab her, his conscience urged. *What else can you do?*

He put one foot forward, and what he heard made him "It" in a bad game of freeze tag.

A raspy sigh, like a throat full of phlegm.

Parker knew he had to act. He took a deep breath, and then, on instinct, charged the double doors. Like a hockey player, he put his shoulder into it, checking them backwards. They closed simultaneously, and as he whirled to reach for Maggie's scruff, the doors rebounded ajar.

The thing within hissed louder, angrier and unfazed.

The moment Parker snatched Maggie's fur her body was ripped from his fingers. He lost his footing and stumbled to the dirt. He watched agape as the gap between the door eased wider and Maggie, with one last yelp, was dragged into the darkness by the skeleton hand.

"No!"

Parker's eyes welled up with tears. He hopped to his feet, fists clenched, scanning the ground for a rock to throw, any kind of weapon whatsoever.

The barn doors slammed shut.

Parker looked up. He felt as if he had been punched in the stomach. Tears spilled down his cheeks. Maggie was inside with that...*thing*. That monster. How was he going to get her out now? How could he have let this happen?

He choked back the sobs, his voice barely above a whisper. "Maggie."

A pool of blood flowed from beneath the doors. Parker shook his head, wiping his tears on the back of his hand. He had let Maggie down. His stupid curiosity had fed her to the barn. And now he could do nothing but watch.

He turned and ran across the field, hoping to make it back home before dark. The horizon had nearly swallowed the sun, and thick shadows crept toward the grove. The more the oncoming eve unsettled him, the faster Parker's legs carried him.

S.D. Hintz

CHAPTER TWO

Pratt Paget stroked his grizzled goatee, then reached over and closed the laptop, perturbed that his writing time had been interrupted. He eyed Parker from head to toe. The boy looked as if he had been dragged through a mud puddle, his sweatshirt redesigned with a skid mark logo.

Pratt removed his glasses and set them on the cluttered desk. "You have absolutely no idea where Maggie ran off to?"

Parker was beside himself. First his mom was too busy unpacking to lend him an ear. And now his dad was personifying the wall. "I told you! That...*thing*...pulled her into the barn!"

Pratt let the word "*thing*" hang in the air. "No one lives on that farm, Park. The owners died over the summer. They just haven't bulldozed the rest of the property."

"But something's there, Dad! I watched it take her! There's blood everywhere!"

Pratt's ears perked at the last statement. He rubbed his eyes, the chaos of the day bearing down on him. He wondered for a split second if Parker had been sneaking peeks at his novels again. He

quickly brushed off the thought. Judging by his son's current state –
red eyes from crying, the high anxiety – it was obvious that
something troubling had occurred. And being a twelve-year-old boy,
scatterbrained at that, he had created a monster, rather than focusing
on logic. A typical child's reaction.

"Muriel!"

"What, Pratt? I told you, I'm not your damn waitress. I've
still got to unpack the clothes, and the comforters —"

"Maggie's run off and we need to find her."

Muriel poked her head around the corner into Pratt's future
home office. Her brunette, curly hair had long lost its bounce,
dangling limply near her crow's feet. Her hands were on her hips
with lips pursed, reloading her verbal machine gun.

"Then go find her. We've been living in the woods for two
hours and the dog's lost? She can't be far. Go with Parker and track
her down. I'll start cooking dinner. And afterwards, you're shutting
off that laptop and helping me clean up this mess."

Pratt stood and gestured at the desk. "It's off. But my
deadline is Sunday. I've still got ten thousand words to —"

"Then I guess you better hurry up. And next time, Parker, when I tell you to take Maggie with you, you put her on the leash. Neighbors or no neighbors, we're still out in the woods."

Muriel reached around the corner into a box, and then threw her husband a flashlight.

Pratt caught it and clicked it on and off, testing the batteries; the light shone strong without a flicker. Muriel turned and walked off toward the kitchen.

Pratt pointed the flashlight at Parker. "We'll take a quick look out there, but if we don't find her, we may have to wait 'til morning."

Parker furrowed his brow. "She's not lost! She's in that stupid barn! And if we wait 'til morning, she'll freeze to death!"

"Calm down, okay? I just don't want you getting your hopes up. What if she's not in the barn? What if she's run off somewhere else?"

Parker gritted his teeth. "She didn't run off."

Pratt rolled his eyes. "Well, let's go see for ourselves, shall we?"

They weaved through the box labyrinth in the living room to the small, tiled foyer. Parker grabbed his blue windbreaker from the brass coat rack. Pratt followed suit, slipping on his leather jacket and zipping it up. They then headed out the front door.

In the few minutes Parker had spent pleading his case, the fiery horizon had been reduced to embers and stars dotted the cloudless sky. A crescent moon hovered like a half-lit chandelier, casting a dim glow on the front yard. Pratt thumbed the flashlight; the cylindrical arc scattered the shadows in its path. He pointed it towards the driveway and nodded.

Parker buried his hands in his windbreaker as his dad led the way two steps ahead. The wind had chilled significantly since sunset, a hint of winter in the autumn air. As they crossed the drive, dust swirled over their feet and the gravel crunched like broken light bulbs. Their evening excursion was already giving Parker goose bumps. The dark turned the trees into extraterrestrial exoskeletons, the shrubs into shrunken heads. The outdoor ambiance made every noise animalistic - the howling wind wolfish, the rustling leaves serpentine. Parker glanced at his dad. The man looked equally paranoid, his eyes darting to every sound and shadow.

They rounded the house. A gust hit them like a passing semi-truck, stinging their bare skin. Pratt tightened his grip on the wobbling flashlight. He scanned the backyard as they continued forward. The lone oak swayed unsteadily, creaking like a rocking chair. The garden netting undulated, as if a giant mole was tunneling back and forth.

Parker was practically stepping on his dad's heels. Second thoughts barraged him. *Maggie's dead. I know she is. After all that blood. What if the same thing happens to us? What's Dad going to do? Write them to death? We should turn back.*

Pratt shivered. "Christ, it's cold. She better damn well be out here. I'm not trying to go on a wild goose chase."

Parker bit his tongue. He wanted to reply with, "Maybe we should just go back inside then," but his common sense got the best of him. There was a chance Maggie was still alive, injured, wondering if he would come back for her. He couldn't abandon her like that. Besides, it would be a sleepless night knowing she was trapped in the barn with that *thing.*

The flashlight revealed the bridge. Father and son stepped up their pace, the cold nipping their napes. They both knew that once they crossed the brook, the field wouldn't be much farther. The grove came into view, the crackling canopy akin to radio static. The wind carried the sound of bubbling water, causing Parker to envision cauldrons, and devil worshippers chanting around fire. He quickly shook off the thought.

Pratt's eyes continued to do the job of ten surveillance cameras, bouncing from thicket to cricket chirp, oak to croak; the slightest movement and sound. As the woods swallowed the horizon, dread crept over him. The last thing on his mind was reenacting Red Riding Hood. He regarded Parker. The boy was nibbling his bottom lip and looking over his shoulder every second. Like father, like son.

They stepped on the bridge side by side. A frigid gust barreled into them. The railings shivered, clinging to the floorboards, as the woodwork creaked like a tire swing. Pratt seized Parker's arm and guided him across.

A splash in the water.

Parker spun on his heels.

Pratt maintained a firm grip, shining the flashlight towards their faces. "It's just a frog. Trust me. I saw them all over the place at the open house."

Parker returned face forward, looked to his dad, then off at the trees. The grove's density had filtered the sunlight earlier, but now, with the wind's help, it shunned the moon completely. Parker only saw pitch-dark and flits of bark, like a brown crayon outline on black construction paper.

This is suicide! There's no way I'm going in there, or letting Dad drag me. If that thing killed Maggie, then it's escaped that junky barn by now. We'd just be walking into a trap.

Parker cleared his throat. "Dad? I don't know about this."

Pratt glared, and his words coated in irritation. "Don't know about what?"

"Maybe we should wait 'til morning."

"Maybe we should let Maggie freeze to death."

Pratt shined a light on the grove. It did little to illuminate their path, like a miner's hat in a cave. Leaves swirled in mini-tornadoes, while the canopy above clashed branches.

Pratt gestured with the flashlight. "C'mon. It's only getting colder…and darker."

Parker reluctantly let his dad lead him into the woods. Almost instantaneously, the gusts faded to a biting breeze. They paused five feet in as Pratt swung the flashlight 180 degrees, their bodies turning with the arc, both praying a wolf or bear didn't come charging forth. Satisfied, Pratt aimed straight ahead and stepped forward.

Branches cracked like whippersnappers, followed by a *whoosh*. A crash resounded, thundering through the ground.

Parker wrenched from his dad's grip.

Pratt seized him by the sleeve of his windbreaker, yanking him back. He scanned their surroundings. "A tree fell, that's it. Just a tree. Probably a woodchuck. Happens all the time. Now let's go. We don't have time for this."

Parker wasn't hearing it. He knew that *thing* was running through the woods, preying on them in the darkness. He'd had enough excitement for one night and was on the verge of emptying his bladder. "I want to go back!"

"If we did that, you'd have nightmares 'til dawn! And we're not even at the barn yet!"

"I don't care! I'm cold! I want to go back! Let me go!"

Pratt let Parker's sleeve slip through his fingers. "Fine! Then go! Tell your mom I went to find Maggie, since no one else gives a damn!"

Parker stumbled out of the woods without another word. Pratt shined the light after him, watching him sprint into the night towards home. He shook his head, cursing under his breath.

He had better things to do than chase his tail, looking for a dog that lacked the common sense to stay by her master's side. He could be dropping another thousand words on *The Closed Casket*. He could be…unpacking.

Anything's better at this point.

He cast the beam on the gnarled bowels of the grove. The wavering silhouettes gave him the willies. And worse yet, now he was all alone. Even the presence of a twelve-year-old boy had given him slight comfort. Regardless of the situation, he walked forward, eyes trained on the only thing that offered consolation – the flashlight.

His mind wandered to the barn, thinking back on Parker's story. *Thing*, that's what he had called it. Not a *someone* or a *somebody*. A *thing*. Pratt recalled him, at one point, referring to it as

31

a "bloody skeleton." The description was odd, certainly a product of adolescence, but what vexed him most was why someone would steal a dog from a kid, inside a barn, at that.

Maybe he's lying, Pratt thought. *Maybe he really lost Maggie. It's not like he had the leash.*

He returned his focus to the grove. He was now at a brisk walk, the darkness yielding a claustrophobic paranoia. He knew he was nearing the field, even though his subconscious continued to suggest otherwise.

He stopped in his tracks as a long, cylindrical object glistened in the path of the flashlight. It was a fallen elm, most likely the one that had scared the crap out of Parker. Pratt walked along the trunk, studying it, running the beam down it like an MRI. He reached the end, resting in a pillow of leaves, and crouched before it.

What the hell?

He expected the breakage to consist of roots and dirt, similar to most trees he had seen on nature hikes that had toppled over mysteriously. But quite the contrary, the end was severed clean, to the point that the rings were visible. The elm had been chopped down.

Pratt's head swam as he stood and scanned the grove, now more paranoid than ever. *That can't be the same tree. There must be another nearby, maybe on the edge of the field. We would've heard someone chopping wood. That's all I need is a demonic lumberjack chasing me down.*

Pratt stepped over the tree and continued on. Twigs snapped beneath his feet. Foliage snagged his jacket. Leaves tickled his face. He suddenly realized he had walked smack-dab into a thicket. He swatted the flashlight like a machete, snapping branches like brittle bones, and forced his way through.

The wintry gust returned with a vengeance. Pratt staggered back a step, clutching the flashlight. He looked up. The darkness of the canopy had receded to the cloudless sky and crescent moon. He had finally emerged from the grove.

He switched off the flashlight, opting to conserve the batteries. The moonlight was ample, almost glaring, given that the field ahead was treeless. The utility fence wobbled ceaselessly, as if locked in an epileptic seizure. Pratt pushed back his jacket sleeve and lit his Rolex. It was 6:43 P.M. Muriel probably had dinner done by now and was worried sick.

Pratt's gaze was magnetic, severing the hands of time and latching on the field. A red glow caught his eye in the distance. He squinted, narrowing his line of sight telescopically. The barn's windows and hayloft surged as if candlelit, looking like a jack-'o-lantern. Someone was definitely inside.

Pratt wrestled his conscience. *Guess the land's been bought since we were last here. And Park's not going to know any different, whether I checked out the barn or not. Trespassing at dusk isn't on my to-do list.*

"Screw it."

If Maggie was inside that barn, at least she was sheltered from the elements. Playing Sherlock Holmes could wait until morning. People were more apt to call the cops at night if someone looked suspicious, rather than the daylight when he could pull off the "leisurely stroll" excuse.

Branches snapped behind him.

He spun, switching on the flashlight. He shined it down the tree line, from left to right. Beyond the rustling elms, the grove was pitch-black…and still. Nothing lurked at the edges, waiting to pounce forth. At least nothing within the ten-foot area of the beam.

Another crackle.

Pratt jerked the flashlight in the opposite direction, scanning slower and lower. Maybe it was something small, like a fox or a skunk, lumbering through the underbrush. But again, nothing jumped out, save for dead leaves caught in the field's tractor beam.

Christ, Pratt, just do one more quick check of the perimeter and get the hell out of here.

For once, he listened to his gut. He stepped into the grove. The moonlight faded like a blown match and darkness encompassed him. The wind died to a slight breeze, which Pratt welcomed, as his hands and nose had gone numb. His flashlight dimmed, and then brightened, a tell-tale sign that the batteries were weakening. He proceeded to swing it 180 degrees, but only made it 70 when something bone-white caught his eye, protruding from behind a tree.

He choked on his words at the thought of calling out, asking if someone was there. The author in him knew you only did that in the horror movies, and it never garnered a response. So, instead, he took another step forward, breaking twigs, announcing his presence even more than the flashlight, all the while staring at the white anomaly.

It's just a mushroom on a tree. What the hell else would it be?

Something hissed nearby.

Pratt turned right, following his instincts. Two beady, yolk-yellow eyes glared before him. He jumped back, startled, and cracked his head on a branch. A burst of pain brought tears to his eyes. He looked up. Besides his pounding heartbeat, the woods were silent. The eyes had vanished.

Another hiss.

Pratt whirled to the left. The flashlight was swatted out of his hands, and flew over his shoulder. He made a half-turn to flee, but something slammed his chin hard, feeling like a heavyweight boxer's uppercut, and knocked him off his feet. He flew backwards out of the grove, landing hard on his tailbone near the fence.

He groaned as his eyes focused on the night sky, the moon shining down like an exam light. He rubbed his throbbing jaw, and realized that his lip was bleeding. He opened and closed his mouth, prodding his gums with his tongue. He was surprised that all his teeth were still there.

A flicker caught the corner of his eye. He craned his neck and saw the flashlight lying in the field, shining toward the barn.

His brain blared a tornado siren. *Grab the flashlight and get the hell out of here.*

He rolled onto his stomach and rose to his feet. The wind howled, shoving him into the fence and rolling the flashlight farther downfield.

Screw it. I'll get it in the morning.

Pratt looked to the grove. The last thing he wanted to do was go back in there. But it was the quickest way home. After all, he was standing in his own backyard. He took a deep breath, clenched his fists, and then sprinted into the trees like he was being chased by a pack of wolves.

CHAPTER THREE

Muriel paled as Pratt shut the door. "You're bleeding! What happened?"

Pratt slipped off his jacket and threw it on the coat rack. "A tree clotheslined me."

"A tree? Have you been out fighting Ents?"

"Ha-ha. Just some stupid branch. That damn grove is off-limits, you hear me?"

"And what reason would I have to go back there? I don't go running around the woods at night."

Pratt kicked off his shoes, banging the closet door. "You know what I mean. I don't want Park going back there."

"Well, tell *him* that. C'mon. Let's eat. We're all starving. The burgers and fries were getting cold, so I popped them in the oven."

Pratt rubbed his chin. The taste of blood still lingered in his mouth. Whatever was in that grove had a mean punch. He tried to shake the image of the yellow, beady eyes from his head; they reminded him of an owl or koala.

Yeah, Pratt, you got the piss knocked out of you by a boxing koala.

Muriel weaved through the maze of cardboard boxes. She looked over her shoulder, eyeing Pratt, her face etched in concern. A dark bruise spanned his jaw. "We should put some ice on that. Are you sure it's not broken? It looks horrible."

"I'm fine. Just a little sore."

"Okay. I asked. At least take some Advil after dinner. You're going to be hurting when you try to shove a burger in your mouth."

Pratt followed Muriel to the dining room, and watched her pass through to the kitchen. He was immediately caught off guard. The hardwood floor was devoid of boxes. So far, it was the only organized room in the house. The oak, two-leaf table glared beneath the golden glow of the brass chandelier. Matching paintings of Italian countryside hung adjacent on the paneled walls. A window with parted, beige curtains provided a shaft of natural light. Pratt eyed the table. The placemats were set and he took a seat across from Parker, avoiding eye contact.

"You didn't find her, did you, Dad?"

Pratt reluctantly looked up. Parker's gaze was narrow, tinged with anger and disappointment. Pratt's mind was still foggy, subconsciously analyzing what might have attacked him. "Find who?"

"Maggie!"

"No, no. She must have run off. Listen. Those woods are off-limits, you got that?"

Parker eyed Pratt's jaw. He had heard his mom and dad discussing the incident in the other room, but was reluctant to believe the details. A branch? It would have to be fairly thick to cause bodily harm.

Parker nodded. "So you checked the barn? She wasn't in there?"

Pratt shifted his gaze from Parker to Muriel as she returned with their plates.

Muriel noted their staring contest, and broke the heavy silence. "What do you guys want to drink?"

Parker looked up. "Milk, please."

Pratt looked down at his cheeseburger and French fries. "Jack and Coke."

Muriel rolled her eyes. She should have guessed. A stiff drink always alleviated his foul mood, and made his family more tolerable. Muriel left the dining room, en route to retrieve the rest of the dinner.

Parker returned his glare. "So? Wasn't she there?"

Pratt took a bite of his burger, his jaw throbbing, and then faced his son's interrogation, which was beginning to make his blood boil. The author in him gripped the mental pen and began reciting an audio book.

"That barn was empty. Nothing but stalls and hay. I checked everywhere, even in the loft, and there was no sign of Maggie. And I don't want you going back there anymore, understand? It's not safe."

Muriel returned with their drinks and her dinner. She then sat down at the end of the table and glanced at her boys. She knew by the expressions on their faces that she had interrupted their conversation. "So, what's the verdict? Did she run off again?"

Pratt took a long sip of his Jack and Coke. "Looks like it. Guess that's why we have that leash, so this doesn't keep happening."

"I'm sure she'll be back in the morning. She probably just got curious."

Parker slammed his fist on the table, rattling the silverware. "She didn't run off! I told you!"

Pratt set down his tumbler, glad the alcohol was quickly numbing the pain. "Now calm down. We all know Maggie will run off if given the chance. This isn't the first time—"

"But you didn't even the check the barn! How could you when the doors are chained up?"

"Now that's enough! If she doesn't come back in the morning, then we start searching every nook and cranny. Right now, it's dark and we don't know where the hell she's at."

Parker opened his mouth to retort, but thought better of it, realizing it was a losing argument. He huffed and stared down at his plate, struggling to muster his appetite.

Pratt sighed as he met Muriel's glare while grasping for French fries. She was giving him the what-aren't-you-telling-me look.

A sudden movement relieved him from optical sign language. His gaze shifted to the window behind Muriel. Between the parted curtains, beady, yellow eyes leered at him. It looked like a floating skull; its head was bald and face rawboned with a flaring, catarrhine-like nose.

The French fries slipped through Pratt's fingers. He knew those eyes. His jaw dropped. The skeletal Peeping Tom mimicked his expression, baring blood red, jagged fangs; its hot breath fogged the glass with every exhale.

Parker looked up from his plate. He furrowed his brows. His dad was wearing a mask of terror, the color drained from his face. Parker followed his line of sight. He froze as icicles slid down his spine. Though he had never laid eyes on it, he knew by its skin-and-bones appearance; Maggie's kidnapper was outside their window.

"There it is, Mom!"

The bone-white trespasser ducked as Muriel turned her head.

"There's what? What the heck are you guys staring at?"

Pratt stood from the table, his mind running rampant. *That was the thing that hit me. That's what Parker saw in that goddamn barn.*

Muriel raised her brows. "Well?"

Pratt pushed his chair back and stood. "Nothing. But I think I forgot to lock up."

Parker hopped up from his seat and pointed accusingly. "But you saw it, Dad!"

Pratt grabbed his Jack and Coke, drained it, and then slammed it on the table. "There's nothing out there!"

He knew those words would fail to convince anyone, but he had to at least try. If Muriel saw what was lurking on the property, she would freak. It had been hard enough to sell her on the idea of relocating to somewhere more isolated.

Pratt turned and walked away from the table. "Sit down and eat, Parker!"

Muriel stood and marched after him. "Pratt! What the hell's going on?"

"It's that *thing*, Mom!"

"Sit down and eat!"

Muriel exited the dining room and spotted Pratt in the foyer, locking the deadbolt on the front door. He then proceeded to draw the curtains in the living room and extinguish the lights.

Muriel was beside herself. Only one other time had she seen her husband react in this manner. Two summers ago, while staying in a cabin on Kettle Creek, Pratt had crossed paths with a black bear in the backyard. He had immediately turned into Security Officer Paget, scrambling to put the place on lockdown, as if that would keep the wildlife at bay.

Muriel weaved through the unpacked boxes. "You didn't run into a tree, did you?" Pratt ignored the question, switching off the lamps one by one. "*Did you?*"

Pratt yanked another pair of drapes closed. "Something's out there, okay? I didn't want to scare you."

"Scare me? You're running around like a tornado's about to hit!"

"Some goddamn thing attacked me."

"What do you mean "*thing*"? What Parker was ranting about?"

"I don't know what it is."

"Stop calling it an "it." Was it a person or an animal?"

"A person, I guess."

Pratt turned his back on Muriel and hurried toward the kitchen. As he passed through the dining room, Parker, sitting in his chair obediently, pointed to the far wall he had been staring at since his parents went into freak mode.

"Dad? What about that one?"

Pratt paused at the archway and looked across the room. He then dashed over to the window and shut the curtains. "Have you seen it out there at all?"

Parker shook his head. "How did it get out, Dad? The barn was locked. If that thing's out there, then Maggie's—"

"I didn't go out to that goddamn barn! That *thing* jumped me in the woods! Maggie's the least of my concerns right now!"

Pratt stormed into the kitchen and locked the back door. He peered out the single-paned glass. The backyard was dark and still as a cemetery, a thin mist roiling through the grass. Pratt's panting fogged up the glass, reminding him of the gaunt trespasser. He suddenly felt like he had been cast with the leading role in a "B" horror movie.

He closed the drapes and returned to the dining room.

Muriel stood in the archway, hands on her hips, blocking access to the living room. "We should call the police."

Pratt rolled his eyes. "The phone won't be activated 'til Monday."

"Don't roll your eyes at me! See? This is why we need a cell phone."

A thunderous, metallic bang resounded outside the house.

The Pagets jumped, and then exchanged fearful glances.

Muriel bit her lip. "What the hell is out there, Pratt?"

Another crash, like a wrecking ball slamming into corrugated steel.

A split-second later, the car horn blared.

Pratt's eyes sparked with anger and his face flushed. The only way the Lexus horn would go off automatically and incessantly was if an impact had occurred with the front end. The trespassing had fueled Pratt's paranoia, but the thought of damage to their personal property pissed him off. He stormed out of the dining room, his brain switching from defensive to offensive mode.

Muriel was still rooted to the floor, her heart pounding like a snare drum. "Pratt!"

In his haste, Pratt kicked over boxes that got in his way, scattering the makeshift maze. His mind was on one track, traveling down one tunnel, on a crazy train Ozzy Osbourne would have been proud of. He made a beeline straight to the fireplace, his first thought in terms of self-defense weaponry. He was immediately grateful for Muriel's organizational skills. She had unpacked the andirons, poker, bellows, and various other accoutrements.

Pratt snatched up the poker and forged to the foyer.

The car horn continued to blare.

Muriel entered the living room. "Pratt! Where are you going?"

"To save the car!"

"The car? What about us?"

"Lock the door behind me."

Pratt barged outside. The car horn drowned out the deadbolt's click at his back. His gaze rode the ear-piercing sound wave. There the Lexus sat in the driveway, gleaming in the glow of the floodlight. A black-tailed deer thrashed against the grill. Its antlers were lodged in the hood, head wrenched backwards, eyes glazed, and body twitching in a relentless seizure. The *thing* stood beside it, looming over it with a bloody axe.

Pratt's lips parted, but his throat was constricted. He wanted to shriek at the sight of the monstrous human, his first good look at it in the light. It was male, bald and easily six feet tall, merely clad in soiled cut-offs. Its body was anorexic and chalk-white; it looked like a skeleton with translucent skin. Pratt's legs were frozen to the front steps. His grip tightened on the poker as he held it before him like a samurai sword.

The skeleton man acknowledged Pratt, flashing a fanged sneer and beady glare. Blood trickled from its blue lips and dripped off its chin. And then, with unexpected strength, it raised the axe overhead and brought it down like a guillotine. Pratt gasped as the blade severed the deer's head in a spray of blood, slamming into the car's hood. The horn died on impact, along with the buck, its body collapsing to the gravel and bleeding out. The starveling wrenched at the axe handle, struggling to free it from the engine block.

Pratt saw his chance. It was now or never. He had to take the madman down before he went Ted Bundy on his family.

He let loose a battle cry and charged the Lexus like a Comanche warrior, raising his fireplace war hawk in the air. The towering starveling released the axe handle, realizing it had become a permanent hood ornament, and turned to confront his attacker. Pratt went for the kill and swung the poker at his skull. The skeleton man sidestepped the blow, his wiry frame swaying gracefully like a sapling. The force of the swing threw Pratt off-balance and his feet slipped in the pool of blood. He belly-flopped on the driveway, his face colliding with the deer's torso as his poker slid into the darkness. He quickly rolled over onto his back, coughing uncontrollably. He gagged, and then forced the vomit down his throat as the smell of fresh kill lingered on his face. He blinked several times and struggled to get his bearings straight. He was beneath the Lexus, his nose inches from the front bumper.

He turned his head and looked beyond the chassis, his awkward position providing a letterbox view. He saw the starveling's bare feet, bloodstained with yellow toe nails, shifting near the driver's side door. He stared down at his shoes as the stick legs rounded the car and stopped before the buck's torso.

Pratt held his breath, hoping the nutcase would forget his whereabouts. All he heard were the starveling's raspy exhales, rattling his rib cage, sounding like the fluttering wings of an injured bird.

Pratt was beginning to feel the gravel poke into his skin, and the smell of motor oil was making his head swim. His jaw throbbed for good measure. He bit his lip, forcing himself to endure the discomfort at least a few minutes longer. His paranoia kicked in as he realized he was a sitting duck.

What the hell is he doing? Is he going to grab me and pull me out from under this damn thing? Or hell, lift the car and slam it down on me?

The starveling's frail hand reached below the grill. Pratt's heart stopped, certain this was the moment he was going to be yanked out by his feet. He watched the long fingers tighten their grip. And then, to his shock, the deer's torso slithered from his peripheral vision, leaving a trail of blood and viscera. He followed the sound of gravel on flesh, like a meat grinder, and craned his neck to the left, back to his letterbox view. The buck slid across the driveway and into the grass.

A light bulb flashed in Pratt's cluttered attic of a brain. He turned his head to the right. There the poker lay, two feet from the car, glinting in the moonlight. Pratt knew he had to act fast while the starveling's back was turned. Like a fish out of water, he attempted a subtle backstroke, pushing sidelong with his palms and heels. The gravel scraped with his movement, and with a final grunt, he slid out from beneath, the gentle breeze chasing away the stench of motor oil.

He gasped, relieved to be free of his claustrophobic surroundings. He rolled over onto his hands and knees. He glimpsed the poker near his foot, grabbed it, and then stood unsteadily, his joints aching from the strain.

A repetitive hissing, like a snake hyperventilating, split the otherwise quiet night. Pratt spotted the starveling rounding the house, the deer torso slung over his shoulder as he sprinted towards the backyard.

Pratt sighed. "Damn."

Hoping their trespasser was fleeing to the barn, Pratt walked to the front of the Lexus. The buck's severed head hovered over the grill, its eight-point antlers jammed through the hood. Its eyes were glazed as blood streamed like a waterfall from its mortal wound to the ground.

Pratt shook his head. *I sure hope insurance covers this. Probably just have to tell them we hit a deer.*

"Pratt! Oh, Jesus! Are you okay?"

Pratt turned and saw Muriel standing on the front step. He nodded. "I'm alright." He gestured with the poker. "Better off than the deer."

"Get in here! I don't like you playing superhero while I worry myself sick."

"Don't worry. The bastard ran off. Took the rest of the deer with him. Look what he did to our car!"

"C'mon already! We'll deal with that later."

"What do you mean? It's not like I can call insurance. The phone's dead."

"Exactly."

Pratt regarded the car, and then decided that Muriel was right. He was out in the open, accomplishing nothing, when he ought to have been inside protecting his family. Playing superhero failed to even earn him a plastic decoder ring. And he lacked the privilege of saying, "Well, you should see the other guy." If he was lotto lucky, maybe the whiff of his swing blew some dust in the starveling's eyes.

Starveling.

Pratt wondered when he had arrived at that namesake. Whatever the case, it was the perfect description. It was a term he had come across while doing research for his novel *The Empty Grave*. "Starveling" referred to a person that was…well…starving.

"Pratt!"

He peeled his eyes off the deer and car, glanced over to the corner of the house one last time, and then heeded Muriel's advice. "Where's Parker?"

"Right behind me."

Muriel stepped aside as Pratt entered the foyer. She closed the door quickly and locked the deadbolt. Pratt set the poker beside the coat track, figuring he could find a smaller, more effective weapon. He would give his gallbladder for a handgun right now.

Parker backed out of his mom's shadow and assessed his dad, who looked as if he was a casualty of war. His face was bloodstained and bruised while his clothes were splotched with dirt

55

and grass stains. His eyes darted over the living room, straining for peace of mind.

"Did you get him, Dad?"

"No."

Muriel had her hands on her hips, wanting answers as well. "Did you at least get a good look at him?"

Pratt's mind was preoccupied, more focused on finding a new means of self-defense rather than twenty questions. He stepped into the living room and opened a nearby box. "Who?"

"Who do you think?"

Pratt sifted through the box. "Oh, yeah."

"*Well? What did he look like?*"

Pratt withdrew a pizza cutter and threw it aside. "A damn skeleton!"

Muriel shook her head. "A skeleton?"

Parker plopped down on the couch, sensing an argument about to erupt. "A skeleton, Mom. I saw its arm come out of the barn. Nobody's that skinny."

"Your dad saw it plain as day, Parker. It's a man, who's obviously homeless and extremely malnourished. Pratt? Pratt!" Pratt stopped rooting in the box and closed the flaps. "You said he took the rest of the deer, right?"

Pratt nodded. "Slung it over his shoulder and ran off."

Parker stood, unable to sit still from all the excitement. His heart was still beating like a mad knocker. "To the barn."

Muriel's nurse skills kicked into overdrive, exploding from a mere spark like dry kindling. "This means he's taking shelter from the cold and living off the land. Pratt, he probably attacked you for a reason. Where did that flashlight go I gave you?"

Pratt sighed and tore open another box. "I lost it. That damn…*thing*…knocked it out of my hands."

"There you go. He wanted the light. I'm sure there's no electricity in that barn."

Pratt bit his tongue upon recalling the red glow that surged from the windows. *The flashlight? No, he wanted something to eat.*

Pratt rifled through the box of tools. A hammer, screwdriver, wrench, tape measure. There had to be something that was as inconspicuous and lethal as a firearm. He knew after this ordeal he was heading to the nearest Wal-Mart for anything with an infrared scope. He shoved aside a metal clamp and found his poison.

Pratt pulled out his FS92 Beretta BB gun and waved it before his bloodied face. It was a gag gift his publisher had mailed him the other week, stating that he would need it for protecting himself in the woods. It looked like the real semiautomatic Italian firearm. It had even been pre-loaded with an eight-round clip, but no extras, as its use was unintended. "I'm sure he's not coming within two feet of this family."

Muriel kicked the box. "Pratt! He's not a monster! He's a human being! He's already suffering and now you want to shoot him to death with BBs?"

"You're damn straight. You saw what he did to the car."

"We need to help him. I'm going out there."

Muriel reached for the coat rack. Pratt grabbed her forearm and pulled her back. "The hell you are. If you want to help him so bad, fine, I get that, but we wait until sunrise. He'll survive one more day in the barn. He's dining on venison for Christ's sake. And I'm not letting you go out there alone."

Muriel looked into Pratt's eyes. Outweighing the terror and paranoia was an immensity of love. She failed to recall the last time she had seen that expression. "Fine. We'll wait until morning."

"I'm barricading the doors."

"They're locked. Isn't that enough?"

"The car was locked. And that didn't stop him from smashing a deer through the hood."

Muriel sighed, long and hard, ensuring her adamant husband heard her dissent. "Parker? Help your dad stack the heavy boxes in the foyer."

"Boxes? We're moving furniture."

"Yeah, Mom. I don't know about boxes."

Muriel snatched the Beretta from Pratt's hands. "Whatever. Build a fortress and dig a damn moat. I don't care. I'm reheating our dinner. Remember? Dinner?"

Pratt rolled his eyes. "Two seconds ago you were so concerned over a starving stranger, now you're hungry? Sorry I'm so *concerned* over our safety."

"Just do it already. And wash up when you're done. You look like a serial killer."

Muriel stormed off through the living room.

Pratt shook his head and looked to Parker. "Help me push the couch in front of the door."

CHAPTER FOUR

Parker grimaced as his dad tugged the deer's antlers. Pratt stood on the bumper, nearly straddling the severed head, gripping the lower, unhindered horns. The blood on the mortal wound had dried, having drained like a downspout overnight. The buck's eyes were vacant and glossed with a yellow film. Its fur wriggled from infestation; every time Pratt wrenched its rack, maggots rained down onto the bloodstained ground. Between grunts and gasps, he cursed under his breath, yet the mounted head refused to give.

Parker rubbed his eyes at the top of the drive. He was exhausted. He had tossed and turned all night, worried the skeleton man would break into their house on a feeding frenzy. The mental images had haunted him relentlessly. The white, bony hand yanking Maggie into the barn. The gaunt, sunken face fogging up the dining room window. Parker eventually passed out face first in a *Spiderman* comic, which had served as an adequate distraction.

"Dad? When are we gonna go check the barn?"

Pratt rocked back and forth on the bumper, slamming the deer's head against the hood. "When I get Bambi out of our goddamn car."

"What if it won't come out?"

"Then I guess we'll have a new hood ornament."

"Will the car still work?"

"It better. Why don't you go help Mom?"

"Why?"

"Because you're not being much help out here."

Parker's shoulders slumped and he turned to head back inside.

Muriel stepped out the front door, untied her grease-splattered apron, and slipped it off. She looked at Parker and gestured behind her. "Breakfast is ready. There's orange juice in the fridge."

Parker mumbled as he passed his mom and disappeared inside. Muriel descended the front steps and paused at the edge of the drive.

Pratt surrendered his tug-of-war and sighed. He stared at the axe. He knew it was covered with the starveling's fingerprints. And now his as well. So much for not disturbing the crime scene. Then again, it was doubtful the police would believe one detail of his story. The moment that he admitted he was a horror author they would think he was telling yet another tale. Or that he was delusional from prescription pain pills. He grasped the splintered handle once more, pushed his toes against the grill, and then yanked hard.

Muriel sighed, catching Pratt's attention. "Why bother? We can call a tow truck Monday."

Pratt released the handle and hopped down from the bumper. "We could. If the phone lines aren't cut."

Muriel balled up her apron. "You can't be serious. This isn't one of your stories, Pratt. I think it's bad enough that you have Parker believing there's a skeleton out here."

"We both saw him, Muriel. The axe isn't proof enough?"

"Of what? That you chopped a deer's head off because it was too dark to see what you were attacking?"

Pratt gritted his teeth, wishing more than ever that Muriel would lay her eyes on their trespasser. "I tried hitting the same thing Parker saw in that barn."

"Which reminds me…After you come inside and eat breakfast, we all need to go out there and find Maggie."

"I know, I know. I'll be right there. I just want to take a quick look to see if that *skeleton* destroyed anything else."

Without another word, Muriel turned and headed inside. It was useless talking to Pratt when something had him distracted. He seemed to erect a soundproof bubble complete with tunnel vision. The rest of the world simply sat and waited until he regained his focus. She had half a mind to mix him a Bloody Mary.

Pratt eyed the grass. A trail of blood snaked from the front bumper of the Lexus to the corner of the house, the same direction the starveling had fled with the deer over his shoulder. He followed it, his sights locked on the crimson stain.

Parker's voice echoed in his head. *A skeleton, Mom. I saw its arm come out of the barn. Nobody's that skinny.*

And that was what baffled Pratt. The thing vaguely resembled a man. Yet as anorexic as said individual was, he had the strength of Mr. Universe. It seemed impossible and was beyond intimidating. What little meat was on his bones must have been muscle.

Pratt followed the blood trail around the corner of the house and into the backyard. He squinted as the rising sun peered between the gray cloud cover. The slight breeze reminded him it was fall and he zipped up his jacket. As he passed the garden, he noticed that the red droplets darkened the farther he traced them, and in spots the grass maintained a trampled imprint, as if the deer had been dragged in places.

His brain ran in circles. *I get that he's hungry, but why is he in the barn? How did he get there? He came from somewhere. Some damn pit to Hell, conjured by a voodoo priest.*

He cursed his overactive imagination. Still, it was a question similar to: "What came first, the chicken or the egg?" Why had the house and silo been razed, but the barn left to stand? He knew he could spend hours contemplating the mystery and arrive at the same dead end conclusion. None of it made a lick of sense.

A hiss stirred the hairs on the back of his neck. The breeze rustled the remaining leaves of the mighty oak, sounding like the starveling. Pratt glanced in every direction, turning 360 degrees, ensuring he was alone.

He returned to connecting the red dots, the splatters darkening to near blackness. Caught up in playing detective, he suddenly realized he had crossed the yard as the crabgrass ended and his shoes hit rotted wood. He stopped and looked up. A dark stain - the remnants of a dried pool of blood – spanned the bridge. Several dead leaves had fluttered into the once-wet fluids and were half-fossilized, fluttering as if waving for help. Amidst all this was the culprit: a pile of intestines still slightly steaming, like a plate of lukewarm spaghetti.

Pratt doubled over the railing and vomited in the creek. The wood supports creaked and swayed, nearly tossing him for a swim. He stepped back, spat, and then caught his breath, fighting off another heave. The smell alone was enough to restart the regurgitation process – a hellish blend of sardines and spoiled milk.

Pratt wiped his mouth on his sleeve and gulped. He eyed the mound of guts; they were too large to be human.

Has to be from that deer. Regardless, I can't have Park and Muriel seeing this.

Pratt kicked the slimy entanglement across the boards. The guts slid off the bridge and splashed below like a cannonball.

Satisfied, Pratt looked over his shoulder one last time, and then crossed the creek. The blood trail solidified, transforming from a splatter to a wavy line, more than likely a result of the disembowelment. It snaked over the leaves and disappeared into the grove.

Pratt sighed. He wished he had his Beretta. It would scare the hell out of anyone by sight alone. At least it was daylight, so the anorexic bastard would have a hard time catching him off guard.

Let's just hope he's nocturnal.

Pratt barged through the dense foliage and froze ten feet in. The slight breeze was heavy with the scent of death. Pratt looked to the ground. The deer's eviscerated torso was sprawled in the underbrush before him. Its mutilated body had served as a wildlife buffet; the flesh was covered in teeth marks from foreleg to hind leg and several ribs had been snapped off.

Pratt took a step back, swallowing his vomit. What sickened him most was the mark left behind by the starveling.

The deer had been skinned.

*****

Muriel glared at Pratt as he entered the kitchen. "Where have you been? Your eggs are freezing."

Pratt avoided eye contact and zoomed in on Mr. Coffee. "Out back."

"In the woods?"

"I ended up there." Pratt paused and poured a cup of Joe. "Our visitor left a trail of blood from the car to the backyard. I followed it across the bridge."

"And?"

"Found the rest of the deer. It was half-eaten…and skinned."

Parker paled. Unbeknownst to his parents, he had returned to the kitchen for a refill of orange juice. He lingered in the doorway, hesitant to interrupt their conversation. His lips parted while his tongue fumbled for words. "It ate…it ate the deer?"

Pratt and Muriel turned.

Muriel replied before Pratt could feed their son's head with more fear. "We don't know that, honey. Don't jump to conclusions."

Pratt sipped his coffee, and then set it on the counter. "He's not jumping to conclusions. I watched that thing decapitate and drag it away. It's common sense."

Muriel glared. "Are you going to eat your eggs or not?"

Pratt looked to the stove. There was a frying pan of scrambled eggs and salsa, long past sizzling. The sight of it made Pratt's stomach turn, reminding him of the deer guts. He looked back to Muriel and shook his head.

Muriel grabbed the pan and dumped the remains in the garbage. "In that case, let's all get our coats on and go look for Maggie."

Parker's eyes widened. Deep down he knew Maggie was dead. The fate of the deer was proof enough. He was scared to leave the house with the carnivore on the loose. "I don't want to go out there. Can I stay here? Please?"

Muriel looked daggers at Pratt before regarding Parker. "No, you can't stay here. You're going to help us find Maggie. You were the last one to see her run off."

"She didn't run off! She's dead! The skeleton man grabbed her and ate her just like that deer!"

"That's enough! Not another word, you hear me? Maggie's out there, alive and well. Now let's put our coats on and get her back. Sitting and supposing only makes me worry."

A tear slid down Parker's cheek. Muriel put her arm around his shoulder and guided him toward the dining room.

"C'mon, hon. We all have to be strong about this."

Pratt left the kitchen, en route to the living room. "I'm grabbing my gun."

*****

The Pagets stepped out the front door and paused at the driveway, scanning the premises. The breeze was back to gusting. The black walnuts rained pale green and chartreuse leaves. The deer head shivered as if nodding, maggots falling from its matted fur. The blood trail stained the ground plain as day from the Lexus to the corner of the house.

Pratt gestured at the gravel. "This way."

Muriel nodded as she grabbed Parker's hand. "Let's go."

Pratt reached inside his jacket and thumbed the Beretta for reassurance. He then led the family across the front yard, walking alongside the red dotted line, feeling as if they followed a treasure map.

"X" marks the spot, matey!

Pratt wished they were searching for gold rather than a dog. Parker had made a valid point. After the deer incident, it was unlikely that Maggie was alive. Of course, Muriel was still the skeptic, but she had yet to encounter the starveling. Pratt wondered how she would react when the curtain was drawn. There was one certainty: it was going to take both of them to keep Parker from turning tail.

71

They rounded the house and were greeted by a glacial gust. Pratt gritted his teeth, all too familiar with Mother Nature's breath, while Muriel and Parker ducked with hands buried in pockets. All three of them had their eyes locked on the blood trail, following it like a homing device as the droplets darkened with each step. Midway through the backyard, Muriel wondered if they were walking along drizzled chocolate syrup.

She silently mocked her husband. *Yeah, maybe Pratt's next novel can be* Willy Wonka in the Woods.

A prolonged creak roused the Pagets from their trance. They paused and looked up. They stood within a few yards of the rickety bridge. The railings swayed like a funhouse contraption. The floorboards had been painted a new red; the crimson blood stain spanned the arch.

Parker's eyes widened. He attempted to wriggle from his mom's grasp, but her grip tightened. "I don't want to go, Mom! Please! Let me go back to the house!"

Parker spun, trying to wrench free, but Muriel reeled him back in like a bass, and then seized him by the forearms. "Parker, listen to me! We need to stick together. If there's anyone out there, we have him outnumbered three-to-one. Now I need you to be brave. Running away isn't going to find Maggie. Understand?"

Parker nodded, shivering once more for good measure. He reminded himself that regardless of how scared he was of going to the barn, it was his idea in the first place. He was the one that had told his folks that Maggie was in there. His mom was right. He needed to muster his courage, and if he saw the skeleton man he could always duck behind his dad for protection.

"The deer's just inside the woods."

Muriel and Parker looked over and saw Pratt on the other side of the bridge, pointing at the rustling tree line. At his feet, beyond the dark stain, the blood splatters merged into a long smear that disappeared into the grove.

Muriel tugged Parker's sleeve. "C'mon. Let's follow the leader."

Mother and son walked side by side onto the bridge, and then parted ways, sidestepping the blood spot. The floorboards groaned like a rotted tree house. Muriel considered grabbing the right railing for support, but had second thoughts as it wobbled in the wind.

S.D. Hintz

Parker glanced over the left rail, and tripped on a knot. He lingered on the arch, his eyes fixated on the stream.

An entanglement of intestines rippled down below, anchored by a large stone and lodged tree branch. Parker's gorge rose at the speed of thought. He looked to his feet. There was a smear from the blood spot to the edge of the bridge. Parker knew that the floating guts had walked the plank...or better yet, been forced overboard.

Muriel paused near the grove beside Pratt and turned. "Parker! C'mon! You can play in the water later."

Parker stepped back from the railing and regarded his folks. His mom's brows were knitted with irritation sewn through her face. His dad's color had drained, and his eyes were wide, lip curled as if to say "I know what you see, but if you say a word, you'll be in the creek, too!" Parker bit his tongue and forced his scrambled eggs back down his throat. He then crossed the bridge, all the while hoping the intestines originated from the decapitated deer rather than an innocent bystander.

Pratt withdrew the Beretta and entered the grove.

Muriel waited for Parker, and then grabbed him by the hand. "From here on out, you stay close to me; no more wandering off."

Parker nodded, his mom's grip offering a slight reassurance. *Wish I could wander off to the house.*

Muriel led Parker into the woods. The shade encompassed them as the wind died to an injured moan. The crisp leaves crunched beneath their feet, announcing their presence to the world.

Pratt stood a few yards ahead, shoulders slumped, unflinching, staring at the ground. The Beretta dangled in his fingers. "It's gone. It was here ten minutes ago."

Muriel paused, clutching Parker's hand. "What's gone?"

"The damn deer. Bastard must've dragged it…"

Pratt's sentence trailed off as his jaw went slack. Muriel and Parker joined his side. An elliptical bloodstain the size of a gravel road rain puddle soaked the dead leaves. A long, dark smear snaked from the spot, deeper into the grove…towards the barn.

Pratt argued with his subconscious. *It was here, skinned and dined on. Maybe when I found it, that starveling was just taking a breather, spying on me from a bush, until I left and he dragged it off. And how do you know a bear didn't come along and grab a bite to eat? There'd be paw prints, that's why. And instead there's…*

Pratt eyed the smear. Sure enough, faint, bloody footprints - *human* footprints – paralleled the trail.

Muriel shook her head. "Pratt? What are you staring at?"

Pratt gestured with the Beretta. "C'mon. We need to hurry."

Parker refused to move. "Mom? I want to go back home."

Muriel yanked Parker forward. "We're not going home until we find Maggie. Pratt? *Pratt?*"

If they were at home, Pratt would have turned the moment Muriel called his name. Truth be told, Parker was scared senseless, and conversing further about the starveling would only make matters worse. So Pratt chose silence, twitched his trigger finger, and marched alongside the crimson smear.

Muriel cursed under her breath. "Great. He's in writer mode."

Parker's eyes bulged. "Writer mode?

"Oh, you know his "writer mode.""

Parker knew his dad's "writer mode" all too well. It was a frame of mind, a "zone" of sorts, with only one focus, while the real world receded into the shadows. When his dad struggled with a concept or was at a loss for words - which was inevitable - he tended to pound his fists, topple furniture, and shout incoherently. Out in these woods with a BB gun, Parker could see him cracking off headshots on squirrels.

Pratt grabbed a low-hanging branch and snapped it off. He then punted a giant mushroom into smithereens. "Dammit!"

Muriel led Parker a good car length behind, like a funeral procession. She glanced at Parker. "I think it's best we give your father some space."

S.D. Hintz

CHAPTER FIVE

While they had been alee within the grove, the moment the Pagets emerged they were shoved back by a gust. They braced themselves and approached the trembling utility fence. Their gazes became binocular, zooming in on the tumbledown barn in the distance.

Muriel looked to Parker, whose hair danced like flames. "So, Maggie's in there?" Parker nodded. "I guess we climb the fence then."

Pratt marched up to the fence, raised his right leg, and booted the top beam. It split in half and thudded on the crabgrass.

Muriel shook her head. "Pratt, that's our neighbor's fence."

"The same neighbor that's running around with an axe?"

Muriel bit her tongue as Pratt stepped over the lumber and headed into the field. A glint caught his eye a few steps in. He crouched and picked up the flashlight. He tested the battery; the beam dimmed, then brightened. He was surprised the starveling neglected to confiscate it. Of course, it probably basked in darkness.

Pratt turned and tossed the flashlight to Muriel. "Lost and found."

Muriel rolled her eyes. "Great. This'll come in handy if there's an eclipse."

"Or if you're attacked."

"Seeing how you have a BB gun, that better not happen."

"Ha-ha. I would've been a sniper if I wasn't a writer."

"Well, then write yourself some instructions on how to fire that thing."

Muriel handed Parker the flashlight. It set her mind at ease knowing Parker had at least some means to defend himself if a situation arose. "Hold this for me. It may be dark in the barn."

Parker nodded. He was certain he would be following his dad's suggestion rather than acting the Boy Scout.

The Pagets squinted in the wind as they crossed the field. Dirt pelted their faces while sandburs clung to their socks and shoes. Parker once again felt the urge to bolt back home, but his mom still clutched his hand. The closer they approached, the larger the barn became, and the more monstrous it appeared. The double doors were like a maw, opening and snapping shut. The meshed hayloft was a cyclopean eye patch. The peeled red paint seemed more like scraped skin.

Parker shivered and dropped the flashlight. *Wait a sec. The doors.*

He eyed the threshold. The rusted chain was on the ground, broken in two. The doors banged open and shut partway, the hinges shrieking like an old swing set. The dark blood smear disappeared within.

"Mom? Maybe I should wait out here."

Muriel shot her son a glare that would have froze Hell. Parker gulped.

Pratt held up his left hand, signaling his family to stay where they were. He sidestepped and looked at the nearest window. It was cracked down the middle and murky as cream of potato soup.

Pratt had hoped to glimpse the interior before they entered blindly, but no such luck. He approached the seemingly endless blood stain. He glanced at Muriel and Parker. "Stay there. I'm just going to peek inside."

Pratt caught the left door as the wind shoved it out. He eased it open while holding the Beretta near his face like a cop's service revolver. He stepped across the threshold and narrowed his gaze.

The barn's confines were gloomy, musty, and smelled of rot. Straw

blanketed the floor. Stalls lined the walls, and all appeared

vacant...except the second one on Pratt's right. There was an animal

shifting, head down, with only its smooth back visible. From Pratt's

vantage point, and the heavy shadows, it looked like a small

horse...or maybe a deer.

A deer, Pratt? Really? Why would there be a deer in the

barn?

A hiss echoed throughout the cavernous confines. Dread

washed over Pratt. He knew that sound. He leveled the Beretta.

There was a starveling in his presence, and the last thing he wanted

was for him to escape the barn.

The animal in the nearby stall lurched forward. The fog of rot

seemed to waft, strengthen. The supposed deer left its sleeping

quarters and turned the corner. Its head glistened pearl white in the

gloom. It straightened slightly, yet maintained its hunched position.

Its beady, yellow eyes flashed upon Pratt. He glanced at the

underbelly below the fur – skin and bones, the physique of a four-

day-old corpse.

Another hiss split the silence. Pratt's trigger finger twitched, nearly popping off a shot. He stepped back and felt the barn doors swing into his heels. The starveling slowly approached, like a timber wolf stalking its prey. He raised his head as he passed beneath a shaft of sunlight filtering through the ramshackle roof. His gaunt face was bloodstained and frozen in a rictus. He bared his jagged fangs, drivel sliding down his chin. The fresh deer skin dangled on his bony shoulders like a crazed shaman.

"Pratt? What's in there?"

The starveling's eyes widened at Muriel's voice. He then leapt like a long jumper with his yellowed claws poised to tear flesh. Pratt's trigger finger squeezed three times. BBs fired blindly as the starveling landed atop Pratt, knocking them both through the double doors.

Muriel and Parker shrieked. Pratt's gun flew backwards as his body smacked the ground. The sudden daylight blinded predator and prey. The starveling rasped and clutched Pratt's throat, his long nails puncturing flesh. Pratt shook his head from side to side, attempting to squirm free. He then yelled and kicked out on instinct. His right foot booted the starveling in the chest. His chokehold snapped and his emaciated body catapulted back into the barn. Pratt scrambled to his feet and shouldered the doors, slamming them shut.

He turned and spotted the broken chain on the ground. He looked at Muriel and Parker, who were frozen in fear. "Hand me that chain! Now!"

Muriel uprooted her feet and heeded her husband. Pratt wound the rusted links around the handles and tied a snug knot. The doors jutted out as the starveling snarled from the other side, yet the chain held fast.

Parker was on the verge of wetting himself. "Can we go back now?"

Pratt turned his back on the doors, satisfied they were locked tight, even as they banged a second time. "Go back and do what? Hide in our house and hope that *thing* doesn't kill us in our sleep? Where's my gun?"

Muriel shook off a shiver. It was her first glimpse of the starveling. Pratt and Parker had been telling the truth. Though instead of feeling sympathy for the malnourished man clothed in deer skin and ragged cut-offs, she was terrified. His teeth had been sharpened inconsistently and the look in his eyes was maniacal.

Muriel turned, crouched and picked up the Beretta. As she stood, she gazed off toward the field. It was deserted, and the grove in the distance waved teasingly. As Muriel spun on her heels, a blur of white glared in her periphery. She paused and cranked her head. A white figure leapt over the utility fence and was sprinting across the field.

"Pratt! I think we've got another problem!"

Pratt regarded Muriel, who tossed the Beretta to him. He caught it and his eyes bulged. While he refused to believe it, it was obvious another starveling was coming to the rescue of his counterpart. "Oh, Jesus."

"Pratt? What do we do?"

Parker knew only one thing to do when he laid eyes on the second starveling: he relieved himself. *Oh my God, we're gonna die.*

The starveling was closing in fast, barreling with its long skinny legs pumping like a track athlete. From where the Pagets stood, minus the deer skin, the emaciated man appeared to be an identical twin. They prayed his personality was the exact opposite. Maybe he was rushing to help his friend out of the barn rather than attack them.

"Pratt!"

Pratt imprisoned his writer's intuition and initiated survival mode. Finding Maggie toppled to the bottom of the agenda as protecting his family became the number one priority. "Back up and move off to the side! I'm going to try to take this guy down!"

Muriel backpedaled with Parker, moving to the left of the barn doors. "How do you know he's coming to attack us?"

"I don't, but I'm also not taking any chances."

"You can't just shoot him—"

"Muriel? That thing in the barn's not coming out to shake our hands!"

Pratt returned his attention to the field. The starveling was less than fifty feet away. His physiognomy and body type were indeed identical. Rawboned, powder skin, hairless from head to toe, beady eyes, and a mouth agape of filed fangs. He hissed like a pissed off python.

Pratt took aim. The Beretta had an eight-round clip and he had expelled three in the barn. If he was lucky, he could take this starveling down with two and have an extra three for the other. He focused on the upper torso, right on the prominent collar bone. When he closed within thirty feet, the starveling let loose a gurgling shriek.

Pratt fired twice. The first BB clipped the starveling's left ear; the second pegged him in the throat, just below the Adam's apple. He clutched both injuries simultaneously, and then tripped over his own two feet, slamming face first into the ground. He moaned and wriggled two yards before Pratt.

Glass shattered, causing the Pagets to jump and whirl in unison. Pratt's jaw dropped as he saw the starveling in the deer skin dive out the barn window and fall atop his wife and son. In that split-second, Muriel reacted on motherly instinct and shielded Parker in her embrace. The starveling collapsed on Muriel's back hissing and rasping. His stench engulfed her – suffocating body odor, copper and hot rotten breath. His bony fingers wrapped around her throat and his nails dug in. Muriel cried out and ducked forward as if about to somersault, flipping him overhead. He landed flat on his back with a gasp.

Pratt ran for Muriel and Parker. The deer skin starveling sat up, leaving his fur on the ground. His back and torso were bloodstained, as if he had been wearing the carcass. Pratt raised the

Beretta and fired. The first shot went wild and knocked out the remaining window glass. The second bounced off the starveling's cheek, bruising on impact. He hollered and clutched his face. Pratt pulled the trigger a third time. The last BB nailed the starveling's hand, causing him to drop it from his injured cheek, shaking it in agony while yelling incoherently.

Pratt reached his family, spun the Beretta and gripped the barrel. He then pistol-whipped the starveling in the skull, knocking him unconscious. His skeletal counterpart coughed uncontrollably.

Pratt turned and saw that the starveling had risen to his feet, but was pained by his bluish-black throat. He looked to Muriel and Parker. He pointed at the glassless window. "In the barn! Now!"

Parker was shivering as if hypothermic. "I'm not going in there! No way! I want to go—"

Muriel grabbed Parker, picked him up, and hoisted him past the sill. He fell to his hands and knees on the straw floor. Muriel then followed suit, grabbing the splintered wood between shards and heaved herself head over heels inside. She landed beside Parker, who was on his feet, absorbing their surroundings. It was dim, musty and reeked like a slaughterhouse.

Muriel stood and eyed Parker. "Where's that flashlight?"

Parker paled. He recalled dropping it outside the barn doors, yet had failed to retrieve it. He pointed at the window. "Out there."

Muriel shook her head. She turned to the window. "Pratt! Grab the flashlight if you see it! It's out there!"

Pratt was on the verge of placing his hands on the sill. He looked over his shoulder. A glint immediately caught his eye. The flashlight wobbled before the barn doors. He looked to the conscious starveling. They locked gazes. The starveling opened its thin lips and ground fangs into gums, sneering as the blood trickled down its chin.

Pratt glanced at the flashlight. It was maybe three yards away, but if he was quick he could snatch it up and dive through the barn window. Or maybe it was better left alone.

Pratt looked back to the starveling, who stood immobile, waiting for him to make the first move. *Screw it.*

Pratt dashed for the flashlight. The starveling sprinted after him. He suddenly felt as if he had started a game of dodge ball and everyone was rushing for the first ball to throw. He reached his goal in no time, grabbed it and spun back the way he came. The starveling slid in his path and swung a right jab, catching Pratt in the temple. Pratt stumbled back and slammed into the doors. The starveling advanced and cocked his fist again. Pratt, with his hands full, could only flail his flashlight and Beretta. And every swing connected. First a flashlight to the jaw, then the Beretta to the opposite side, and three more hits apiece until Pratt saw his escape route. He ran past the bleary-eyed starveling toward the windowsill.

The starveling squinted through tears and rasped. He seized the door chain and wrenched it free, untying the knot with inhuman strength. He then chased after his prey.

Pratt reached the window, panting, and tossed the flashlight and Beretta inside.

Muriel rushed over and grabbed his wrists. "Pratt! Hurry up and get in here!"

Pratt grasped the sill and pushed himself up, grunting. "Move back!"

As he leaned forward to lunge inside, a hard object smashed into his head, clearing him away from the window. He landed shoulder first on the ground and rolled to his back, staring at the blue sky. His entire head throbbed, and he felt a goose egg forming. He clung to consciousness as the starveling filled his vision. The chain dangled in his bloodstained hand. He clubbed Pratt once more, dealing him a blackout. He then bound Pratt's ankles and proceeded to drag him alongside the barn.

Muriel ran to the window. It had all happened so fast. One second Pratt was climbing inside, the next he was gone. And then the starveling passed by. She looked to the right and saw him towing Pratt by his ankles with a rusted chain, heading towards the corner of the barn.

"Pratt! Let him go, you bastard!"

CHAPTER SIX

Muriel lost it and collapsed to the straw floor, sobbing uncontrollably. She was terrified and helpless. All she had now was Parker, a flashlight and an empty BB gun. Her beloved husband had been taken away. He had looked dead, but she prayed he was merely unconscious and that the starveling was not a cannibal. He had to be alive, and she had to act fast. Besides, they were sitting ducks in the barn.

Parker put his arms around her shoulders and held her. "Don't cry, Mom. It'll be okay. Dad will be okay. Right?"

Muriel nodded. She sniffled, regained her composure. She then took a deep breath and met Parker's frightened eyes. She knew she needed to be strong for him. She hugged him hard and then stood unsteadily. "Grab that flashlight and turn it on."

Parker obeyed and shined it on their confines. There were six stalls on each side, all seemingly unoccupied. A wood ladder leading to the hayloft dangled near the back. There was a square hole in the center of the floor. Above, something hung from the rafters, maybe an animal, reminding Parker of a piñata.

Muriel followed the flashlight, contemplating their situation. "Let's check the stalls. Look for anything we can use as a weapon."

They walked together, cautiously, hoping they were alone in the barn. They passed the doors, which banged in the wind, prompting Muriel to realize that they were unchained. She knew they had to find a means of self-defense fast. They arrived at the first stall and Parker cast the beam on it. The shadows retreated, revealing a pile of bones and tufts of fur scattered about.

Goose bumps sprang on Parker's arms. "I don't like this, Mom. I think we should find dad and get out of here."

"We find a weapon, then we can find—"

A window shattered behind them, and a body rolled across the straw floor. Parker, hands trembling, shined the flashlight on it.

"Pratt! Oh my God! Are you okay? Are you hurt? Oh thank God!"

Pratt wriggled and moaned. He slowly sat up, panting. Shards of glass fell off his jacket to the floor. His forehead was bleeding, his face was cut and he had a black eye. "I'm fine. Bastard tried to drag me to some drainage ditch. I guess he planned on drowning me."

"But what happened? Where'd he go?"

"I got loose, landed a punch on him. Then he picked me up by the throat and threw me into the window. Christ, I need a real gun."

"C'mon, get up. Parker and I were trying to find some weapons. There has to be something we can use."

"Is there another light? Last night I saw a red glow coming from the windows."

Pratt grabbed the flashlight from Parker and shined it near the doors. He spotted a string dangling down a nearby post. He walked over and pulled it. A click resounded and a light turned on, casting a crimson glow on their confines. Pratt looked up. A bare, bloodstained 100-watt bulb swayed just below the rafters, tickled by the wind from the hayloft.

Pratt turned off the flashlight and tossed it back to Parker, who caught it by the head. The Pagets then scanned their surroundings, walking side by side, glancing about warily. The straw floor was blood-splattered from wall to wall. Every stall they passed was littered with bones or cow skins, but lacking any remnant of flesh. It was obvious the starvelings had turned the barn into a buffet.

Parker's gaze locked on the animal dangling above. It hung five feet below the red light, its features accentuated like photographic film in a darkroom. Though it was small, Parker knew it was not a goat or pig. Its ears were floppy, fur smooth, and tail long. Its tongue lolled between its canines. It was Maggie.

Parker dropped the flashlight. *"No! No! Maggie!"*

Pratt and Muriel snapped their heads. They spotted their Golden Retriever hanging by her rear paws, bloodied and disemboweled. Muriel ran to Parker and embraced him as he sobbed. Though he suspected Maggie had fell victim to the starvelings, seeing her dead body was a punch to the gut. All his hopes were smashed to oblivion. And the more he cried in his mom's arms, the angrier he became.

"They're gonna…pay for this, Mom. They killed her. They killed my Maggie."

Muriel held Parker to her chest and muttered condolences. Pratt tore his eyes off the dog and focused on the hole in the floor. A heavy stench of rancid meat emanated forth. A broken, rusted latch protruded at the edge. Beyond the pit, a trapdoor laid flush against the straw, the cedar boards covered in claw marks.

Pratt approached the lip and squinted below. Though the light above was bright, the bottom of the hole was buried in darkness. "Muriel. Throw me that flashlight."

Muriel kissed Parker's forehead, fetched the flashlight and lobbed it. Pratt caught it and switched it on. The shadows scattered like startled cockroaches. Pratt fought a dizzy spell as he stared at the macabre hole. The walls and floor consisted of black dirt. A ladder of yellowed femurs descended the far side. Two human skeletons sat shoulder to shoulder. Stones shaped into crude arrowheads littered the ground amongst gnawed animal rib cages and skulls. A pitchfork, trowel and spade were piled in a corner.

Pratt's head spun. *Human skeletons. But whose? And arrowheads. Either they're Indians or they've been sharpening things…like their teeth.*

Two bangs echoed throughout the barn.

Pratt whirled and lost his footing. He slipped on the lip of the hole and went down. His chin caught the trapdoor latch, slamming his already bruised jaw. He freefell ten feet and landed on his back, hitting his head on the floor. He lost consciousness on impact.

Muriel and Parker had turned at the bang as well. The twin starvelings stood at the double doors, rasping. Their skin looked dark red in the barn light, as if they had drenched themselves in buckets of blood. The left held the chain in both hands while the right clenched and unclenched his fists, strangling an invisible victim.

Muriel glimpsed Pratt falling into the pit and gasped. She looked to Parker and pointed to the hayloft. "Get up that ladder! Now!"

Parker bolted on command. He wasn't about to play tug-of-war with the stickmen again. He hopped onto the ladder and clambered up. He peered over the top rung, suddenly paranoid that there could be another starveling hiding upstairs. He sighed. The hayloft was deserted. The wire mesh window fluttered in the gust. The room itself was bare, merely three walls and a straw floor.

Parker crawled over to the window. He was about to look outside when a glare caught his eye. Four black-and-white photographs were nailed below the sill. Parker studied each one from left to right. The first: a family portrait, a farmer and his wife flanked by their two taller sons, arms over their shoulders. The second: the two brothers, more frail, their hair thinner, spreading straw in the barn with pitchforks. The third: a vertical shot outside a window, as if spying, the starvelings – Parker was positive it was them, the siblings – clad in rags, wrestling a calf to the ground. And the last: an interior close-up of a clearing in the straw - the trapdoor, shut and locked tight. Parker lifted up the second picture and looked at the other side. Written in pencil was the phrase *Owen and Ollie, June, 2011*. It was dated three months ago. Curiously, Parker flipped over the last photo. Another caption: *When the scorner is punished, the simple is made wise.*

Parker began to fit the pieces of the puzzle. *It sounds like a Bible verse.* He looked to the family portrait, then back to the trapdoor photo. *Their parents must've locked them in there. 'When the scorner is punished…' Whatever they did, it was something really bad. Maybe they killed that cow in the picture. Or some other animal. And they deserved it…for killing Maggie.*

A bang shook the hayloft, startling Parker. He scrambled to the edge, heart thundering. Below, one starveling whipped his chain like a mace against an upright, snapping it in half. The other hissed and made fists, cracking his knuckles in anticipation. They both advanced toward Muriel.

Pratt came to. He groaned and blinked his eyes back into focus. *What the hell?* The flashlight lay on the floor, shining in his face. He grabbed it and slowly sat up; his back screamed from his nape to his tailbone. He gritted his teeth and inspected the hole.

"Pratt!"

Muriel's cry was a blunt reminder of his situation. He saw himself falling back as the starvelings entered the barn. And then blackness.

The flashlight uncovered the pile of farm implements in the corner. Pratt stood and tossed all three above. He then grasped the femur ladder and scaled it.

Muriel's head snapped at the clangs. She spotted the pitchfork, trowel and spade beside the trapdoor. She looked to the starvelings. The brothers had them trapped. Their only choices were to fight them off or jump out a window. Muriel knew that running was a temporary solution. She glanced back to the farm tools; she had to make a move for them, it was her only means of self-defense. Her gaze shifted. The starveling with the chain swung again and broke another upright. The barn groaned like the belly of a famished dinosaur. The twin was bug-eyed and drooling, hissing, staring at Muriel as if she was a piece of meat.

Pratt climbed out of the hole, caught his breath. He turned and saw the starvelings closing in. He locked eyes with Muriel. He looked to the floor. The rusted tools were at his feet.

Sensing danger, the starvelings sprinted toward their prey. Pratt snatched the spade and chucked it to Muriel. She caught it by the handle and swung as her unarmed predator reached for her throat. The flat blade smacked him in the hands, snapping his wrists back. He howled and stumbled aside into a stall.

Pratt picked up the pitchfork a second too late. The moment he crouched, the starveling's chain uppercut him. He dropped the weapon and fell flat on his back. The skeleton man continued to windmill his steel whip, his toothpick arms spinning with the strength of gears.

"No!"

The starveling spun and targeted Muriel with the spade over her shoulder in a clubbing position. He let the chain fly, launching like a cobra's head, and it slammed into her gut. The spade thudded on the ground as she doubled over and fell to her knees. The starveling hissed in glee. His brother lumbered out of the stall, clenching and unclenching his hands. They eyed each other and then approached the Pagets, eyes beady and burning with hate.

Parker was still watching the events unfold from the hayloft. His mom and dad were stirring, struggling to ignore their pain and stand. He knew he had to create a distraction and buy them some more time.

"Owen! Ollie!"

The starvelings looked up at the hayloft. Their eyes glazed upon hearing their names, as if recalling their past lives. Owen regarded Ollie's hands, and then nodded at the ladder. Ollie hissed and obeyed.

Owen was on the verge of returning his attention to Pratt and Muriel when the chain was yanked from his hands. He spun on his heels, mouth agape, flashing his severed tongue and bloodstained fangs. Pratt smirked. He snatched the pitchfork at his feet and tossed it to Muriel, who in turn dashed for the hayloft.

Pratt saw red. First the starveling killed and gutted Maggie, then attacked Muriel and him with the same intentions. It was downright animalistic. No doubt the crazies would resort to cannibalism in a heartbeat. Pratt was going to ensure they never left the barn again.

Muriel's gaze locked on the ladder. Ollie had clambered to the top rung, quick and agile as a monkey. Rasping, he peered over the edge of the hayloft.

Parker stood near the mesh window, teary-eyed and trembling. "You killed Maggie!"

He ran at the starveling and booted him in the face. Ollie's body launched backwards off the ladder and plummeted. Muriel watched, relieved, as he fell the extra mile into the hole. She winced at the crunching thud, and then exchanged slight smiles with her courageous son.

Owen screamed at the top of his lungs, knowing in his heart that a piece of him had died, his twin brother, his sole companion in the pitch-black of the trapdoor.

Pratt tested the chain's weight, and guessed it at about ten pounds, heavy but manageable. Owen, armed with only his fangs and claws, rushed Pratt, still belting a ceaseless battle cry. Pratt heaved the chain overhead and swung it. Owen ducked beneath the arc as it collided with another rotted post, smashing it to pieces.

A groan reverberated throughout the barn – wood and metal grinding apart. The walls shifted six inches. Windows cracked and shattered.

Owen tackled Pratt to the ground. The starveling punched him in the eye, and then wrenched the chain from his grasp. As Pratt lie stunned, Owen wrapped the chain around his throat, cutting off his airway.

Parker yelled from above. "Owen! Owen! Up here!"

The starveling twitched at his name, but refused to let it distract him. Pratt, face turning blue, gasped for air. He flailed his left hand and found a nearby object. He knew what it was at the touch. He felt his consciousness fading as he gripped the handle. He mustered his remaining strength and buried the trowel into Owen's right cheek. The starveling yelled, releasing the chain. His hands shot to his bleeding face and tugged at the handle.

Pratt scrambled backwards on his elbows and spine, dragging the chain with him. Owen stood and removed the trowel, blood gushing from the wound as his cheek dangled like chicken skin. His eyes bulged and locked on Pratt, burning with vengeance. He raised the trowel and advanced, arm cocked in a tomahawk chop. Pratt grabbed an adjacent post and pulled himself up. He unwound the chain from his throat.

Owen hissed like a gas leak, unrelenting. He then hacked, and gurgled, and coughed a wad of blood at Pratt's feet. He looked down, dropped the trowel, and clutched his stomach. He slowly turned, wobbling, wondering of the culprit as anger and pain poured through his veins. He felt like a hog on a spit impaled on the pitchfork.

Muriel stood there, trembling from head to toe, stone-faced and leering, her nurse sympathy a phantom emotion. She clutched the spade in her other hand. Tears streamed down Owen's face as blood poured from the intestinal wound. He hissed, rasped, gurgled. In a last ditch effort, he lunged toward Muriel, hoping to pierce her chest with the tines. But she had read his intentions. She swung the spade like a baseball bat and connected with his head, knocking him into a backpedal. He collided with Pratt, who grabbed onto the pitchfork handle for dear life. Both men smashed through the post and stumbled, their feet entangling. Pratt landed on his back hard, with Owen on top of him, skewered. The starveling's body slid down the length of the pitchfork, resting on Pratt, feeling like the weight of three comforters. He quickly shoved the starveling aside, doing his best to avoid the blood streaming from the mortal wound.

He sighed, and the barn moaned. Two posts on the opposite end snapped.

Muriel whirled and was relieved to see Parker scrambling down the ladder. "Hurry! We have to get out of here!"

She grabbed her son and husband's hands and dashed for the doors. The entire barn shrieked, sounding like a tank slowly getting crushed in a compactor. The moment the Pagets reached the threshold, the hayloft detached and the red light extinguished, slamming down on Owen and the trapdoor. Muriel tripped on the uneven field and fell, dragging her family to the ground face first. They all quickly rolled onto their backs, ensuring they were at a safe distance. Muriel put her arms around her men as they watched in silence.

The barn collapsed like a house of cards. First the walls, caving into a "V" shape, the remaining windows imploding. The Pagets could hear the inner uprights snapping like bones. The roof buckled and folded in on itself, crashing down and flattening the rest of the skeleton, riling up a dust cloud that engulfed the cacophony for a good twenty seconds before settling.

Parker thought back on the photos in the hayloft as his awe of the structural failure faded. He spoke his mind, muttering. "They were twins. I think their parents locked them in that hole." He paused, recalling the handwritten captions. "*When the scorner is punished, the simple is made wise.* That's what one of the photos said in the hayloft. "

Muriel shivered at the thought, but she knew her son was telling the truth. Owen and Ollie had been traumatized and on a rampage, as if locked up and starved. The caregiver in Muriel resurfaced. How could a parent do such a thing to their children? Whatever their misdeed, confined beneath a barn trapdoor was an unforgiving punishment.

Pratt dwelled on the hole while considering Parker's statement, most importantly the biblical quote which he knew all too well. He recalled the human skeletons, arrowheads, and animal bones. His conclusion was straightforward. The parents had locked their children in the hole for some minor misbehavior. And naturally, the kids had shaped stones into arrowheads and sharpened their teeth to fangs, possibly to consume whatever farm animals had been left with them. Then at some point – *those human skeletons* – the parents had returned, maybe out of guilt, or to lift their grounding, and the starvelings sought vengeance, eating them alive. Pratt had his next novel outlined. Funny thing was his publisher and readers would never know it was nonfiction.

"Muriel? All those boxes you unpacked…"

Muriel was nodding. "I'll be a packing machine."

Parker jumped on the bandwagon. "I'll help, too, and load 'em back in the car! Can we stay at a hotel tonight? One with a pool, and a waterslide?"

Pratt stood and pulled Muriel and Parker to their feet. "A hotel sounds good. We won't be coming back here again. I don't need this place to help me write my next novel. I just need a Jack and Coke."

Muriel squeezed Pratt and Parker's hands. "You fix a drink. I'll drive us the hell out of here."